The Rainbow

A story of romance and discovery

By: Larry O. Bubar

Illustrated by: Lynn Cote

Published by:
  LB Books
  Box 844
  Presque Isle, Me. 04759

        isbn 978-0-6151-6198-3

This book is dedicated to
romantics regardless of
age

Also to my wife Takiko and
my friend Gayle

(I would also like to thank Wendy and Vince
for their help with editing.)

I
We Begin

Rainbows seem to be such magical things. They shoot across the sky in bright hues after the rain. There are many myths about the rainbow. Some believe that at the end they will find a pot of gold or some other treasure. Others believe that the One known as God sends it each time it rains to renew His promise of never flooding the earth again. Still others believe that it holds great powers, of one kind or another, to heal, to grant wishes, to transform one from one realm to another, or that is possesses the true entity of love.

Now on most accounts I yield to the wise masters in the area of their belief but on the theory of it holding the entity of love I think I can shed some light on the subject. For it is an ancient tale of a young boy and his undying love for a princess that bears witness to the rainbow's power in this field.

Many eons ago in an ancient land, where Mongolia now exists, was a kingdom ruled by the Emperor Mang. A good enough guy, as emperors go, but very controlling of his children, especially his daughter Wei Wu. In a remote village on the far side of the kingdom lived the Chan family. Yi Chan, the father, was by trade a maker and displayer of fireworks or as they called them, the bursting stars of night. He would travel around from village to village putting on displays for festivals, weddings, and even funerals. The trade of displaying starbursts went back five generations and Yi hoped that it would continue for at least five more.

Yi was known far and wide as the greatest master of the bursting stars. On his travels a young lad was seemingly always present by his side. The boy, called Yin, would dutifully assist his father at the trade, learning all he could in order to take his father's place when the time came.

Yi and Yin watching the starburst (fireworks)

Yin had one other passion and that was archery. He would practice ever minute he could slip away and in time became quiet proficient at it. Soon he was entering the local festival archery contests to while away the time before the big show. In time he was a force to reckon with, for he won many contests and the prizes of food stuff or clothes and on rare occasions small bits of money. All of which he gave to his family as his contribution to their being.

II
The Invite

Time passed and Yin grew from a young lad into a young man. He traveled far and wide throughout the kingdom with his father putting on shows. His ability for working the bursting stars was becoming well known, second only to the skill of his father. His superb talent with a bow was also well known almost to the level of legend. So it wasn't a surprise when Emperor Mang chose the pair to provide the entertainment at his daughter's fifteenth birthday. Now fifteen, to children of the kingdom, was special for it marked the last day of childhood and the beginning of their life as adults and the time to think of marriage, especially for women.

Yin and his father worked hard each day well into the night getting ready for the great festival of the Emperor Mang. What an honor that had been bestowed upon them. This would cement their names in the great stories for generations to come. Few people throughout the realm were given such honors and Yi did not want to waste the opportunity.

They arrived two days early to ensure all preparations were completed in time and that all was just right, for to disappoint the Emperor would surely mean chastisement or even exile. On the second day, when Yin's father had determined that all was ready, he told Yin that he could have the rest of the time, until the show, to explore the village and take in some of the local sights and culture and maybe even enter the archery contest scheduled for that afternoon.

III

Yin sees Wei

Yin wasted not a minute and was off at a run. He wandered the streets and alleys tasting exotic foods and watching street players perform their acts. There was the fire eater, the snake man and the lady that seemed to float in the air. He saw great treasures from the far corners of the globe: fine silks, copper ware and jewels so bright that the sun paled in comparison. Yin lost track of where he was and soon found himself in a part of the village away from the main area. He sat on a rock trying to figure out where he was and better yet how to get back to the center, for surely his father would be wondering where he was.

It was faint at first, almost a whisper, then the volume increased and he recognized it as a giggle of a young girl. It had seemed to come from behind the wall that stood behind him. Intrigued, Yin approached the wall trying to find out from whom the giggle came. As he approached the wall, the giggling got louder and he was then sure that it was a young girl and another person that sounded much older.

He spotted a window sort of hole in the wall and, as luck would have it, a rock was just beneath it. Standing on the rock he could easily see through the hole to what lie behind the great wall. It was a garden sort of place with many flowers, a pond and well-kept lawns. Surely this had to be the inner garden of the Emperor's home, for no other place in the kingdom could be so grand. Then she caught his eye. A young girl, no a young lady, sitting on a bench with an older woman. They were wrapping colored flowers around a stick. "Probably some decoration for the big gala that night," he thought. But his eyes couldn't help but stay fixed upon the girl's face.

Wei in the garden

Such beauty he had never before seen anywhere in his travels. Big, bright eyes, long jet black hair glimmering in the sun, skin smoother than that of a baby, and a smile that would ignite the hearts of all that seen it. He must have stood there forever just staring at her beauty when he was snapped back to reality by a voice.

"You boy, what are you doing?"
"I could have you beheaded for looking in here," the voice said half serious and half in a jest.

"Ah looking for my lost bird," he stammered. It was all he could think of at that moment.

"Well, you best be off before the guards find you and toss you in the pit," said the voice. In an instant he was off and running, not stopping until he was safely in his room.

IV

Awaiting the Show

His father noticed the pale look on Yin's face. "What's the problem Yin?" he asked.

"Ah nothing father," was the reply.

"I can clearly see that something is bothering you son," the father said.

"Well, father I just saw a vision of the goddess Yoa right here in this village."

His father gave a slight laugh and replied "You know that Yoa is a myth as well as I do."

The young lad laughed too and shook his head in agreement. "I know father but I swear I saw her this very day in the palace garden." Yin then related his adventure of the afternoon.

After he finished, his father smiled and said "Well maybe so, my son, but seeing behind the palace walls can only get you into deep trouble."

Again Yin nodded. But still Yin thought it was worth the chance he took. "Seeing the girl for one moment of time was worth all the trouble it could bring," thought Yin to himself.

Yin spent the rest of the day sitting around thinking of the young girl he had seen earlier. It consumed his every thought, so much so that he missed lunch and dinner. He even forgot about the archery tournament that offered many great prizes.

He was brought back to reality when he heard his father say "Come on Yin or we'll be late for the show and we surely don't want to disappoint the emperor."

Knowing the girl would be at the show, Yin leaped up and practically dragged his father out the door. As was the case with a Yi show, it went off perfectly with many bright color bursts and many fancy, spectacular mini-shows. The emperor was so impressed he invited Yi and Yin to the gala feast being held in the grand hall. Yi tried to beg off, but the emperor would not hear of it. Yi, sensing that Yin wanted very much to attend, finally relented and agreed to attend.

V

The Gala

There was plenty food and drink and acrobats and songsters present. Yin paid no attention to any of that; his focus was only on the young girl sitting next to the emperor. "Isn't she the most beautiful girl ever?" he asked his father.

"Who?" was the reply.

"The princess," Yin answered.

"Oh yes she is a beauty," Yi replied. "But you best be careful. She's way above your station and her father would behead you if he caught you near her."

Yin laughed and said, "I can take care of myself but thanks for worrying about me."

Yin pretended he didn't care about his father worrying about him but he really did appreciate his concern.

Soon a hush came over the hall as the emperor stood and offered a toast to his daughter that was now a woman. Then he said "It is time for her to choose the one with whom to start the dance."

The princess stood and searched around the room until her eyes stopped at Yin.

She said "I choose the starbuster's son."

Many in the hall gasped at her choice but her father laughed a little and asked "Are you sure?"

"Yes," was the reply.

"So be it," said the emperor with a chuckle.

So Yin and Wei met in the hall center and the music started. Yin had no idea how to dance and when he started the hall became an uproar of laughter.

"Pay them no mind," said Wei. "They are just jealous snobs."

Wei took his hand and showed him the steps and he followed quite nicely.

"I am Wei," she said.

"I am am am ah," was all Yin could sputter out.

"You're Yin," she said with a laugh and a smile brighter than a million stars.

"Yes, I am," he stammered.

"I saw you at the garden wall today," she said.

"Ah yes, and I'm sorry to have bothered you," he replied.

"Oh I thought it gallant and brave of one to risk beheading just to peek over a wall," she said.

"Well, I was looking to see where the laughter was coming from," he replied.

The dance ended and before she returned to her seat she leaned over and whispered in Yin's ear. "Come again tomorrow at noon. I'll be waiting by the same hole as you were peeking through today," said Wei with half a laugh.

Yin tried to think of something gallant to say. Wei chuckled and bowed, then she was off to her father's side. "I will," he finally whispered to the empty air.

She must have heard him for she turned and smiled. The smile sent cool goosebumps all over Yin's body. He couldn't help but smile in return.

Yin and Wei dancing

VI

Yin Makes a Decision

The next day Yin was very restless and had a hard time helping his father pack up their equipment.

"We must be off soon," said his father.

"Oh no father we can't leave until after the dragon dance show and that is late in the day," Yin blurted out.

"Why is that I didn't know you like the dragon dance show?" asked Yi.

"Well one can never get too much culture now can they?" asked Yin.

"I guess not," said his father with a suspicious tone.

At noon Yin rushed to the garden wall and peeked through the hole as he had done the day before.

"Boo," said a voice as Wei appeared on the other side of the hole

"I'm glad you came," she said.

"Me too," was the reply.

They talked for what seemed like a century yet was only a few moments.

They heard a voice call "Wei Wu where are you, come on its time to go in."

"Coming," she replied.

"I have to go before she comes and finds you here" Wei said.

"Oh, please just a moment longer," begged Yin.

"I can't. If she finds you here she'll tell my father, and then you'll be in trouble, for he is a very quick tempered man," said Wei.

"I fear him not, for you I'd gladly take that chance," replied Yin.

"Silly boy," she said with a giggle and was off at a skip.

Yin met his father at the show and his father, knowing where he might have been, asked no questions. "Father do you think me old enough to be on my own?" Yin asked.

"Well sure, son. You are a young man capable of such," replied his father.

"Why do you ask?"

"Well, I was thinking of staying here in the village for a while and see what it's like," replied Yin.

"Ah foolish boy it's the girl talking not you. You would have no chance to woo her and if her father found out he would surely have your head," said Yi.

"I know father but I must chance it I would be untrue to my feelings if I didn't," said Yin.

"Well, what will you live on?" asked Yi.

"I will find work. There must be someone needing extra help, harvest time will soon be upon us," replied Yin.

Yin's father knew what was in the boy's heart, but felt it a large risk for him to take. Yi and Yin talked more of the plan until finally Yi realized he was on the losing end of the conversation. So with a heavy heart, filled with some fear, he agreed to let Yin stay but only until the late winter festivals, and then he'd have to return to help with the shows. Yin, knowing that he could only push the subject so far agreed to his father's proposal. They finish watching the dragon dance show and Yi prepared to leave. For the first time he ever could remember he was leaving Yin behind.

"Have a safe journey," said Yin.

"Ah yes I intend to and you keep that head on your shoulders. I can't have a headless boy helping me set up the star burst."

"Ok father I'll do that," replied Yin with a chuckle.

Yin and Yi talked some more about what Yin could do to survive in the village.

Yi said "Now whatever you do don't get caught up in the village life and forget where you came from," said Yi.

"Have no fear father I won't," replied Yin.

Yin's father reached into his purse and withdrew a few coins and handed them to Yin. "Here this should get you by until you find work," said his father."

"Oh no father I couldn't. You need that to live on," replied Yin.

"We will manage; and besides you have earned it, count it as your first pay from a job," said Yi.

Reluctantly Yin took the coins feeling both unworthy and grateful. His father said a final good bye and hugged him, then was off to the home that Yin had given up, at least for a time.

VII

Yin Courts Wei

Yin found several jobs helping the locals for a day or two at a time. When he could, he'd sneak over to the wall and see if Wei was there. They would talk for several minutes before the familiar "Wei it's time to go" was heard. About two weeks into his stay, Yin got a break that he couldn't believe. The royal gardener offered him a job as an assistant in the palace garden. This was the luckiest thing to ever happen to the lad. He could be in the palace and see Wei without being suspected by anyone. So each day Yin would clean the grounds, prune the trees and skim the fish pond. At noon time he would go to the section where Wei's escort taught her to read. He would sometimes get to speak to her for a short period. In time, it seemed when he arrived the escort would think of something she had forgotten and would go inside to retrieve it. This left the two young ones alone. They would talk about their dreams. What they hoped for in the future for themselves and the kingdom. On some occasions, they would even hold hands but very secretive as to not cause trouble. A book placed over them or a scarf and sometimes an umbrella, but they were always careful. When the escort returned, having found her misplaced item, Yin would quickly return to work. He knew the escort did it as a favor for Wei, for no one forgot that many things, but he was thankful she did and also that she told no one. One day, while Yin and Wei were talking, the escort came back in a hurry.

"You leave quickly," she panted.

"Why?" Asked Yin with a perplexed look.

"The emperor is coming to see his daughter," said the escort.

"Hurry lad hurry" she coached.

But it was too late. The next sound they heard was. "What is this knave doing here with my daughter?" roared the emperor.

"I was just fixing the bench for her sire," replied Yin.

"You think me a fool lad?" shouted the emperor.

"No sir not at all," stammered Yin.

"Guards take him away. I'll deal with him later," said the emperor.

"Please father, no. Pease let him go, he did no harm," begged Wei.

"Quiet daughter. You don't know what is in the hearts and minds of such young men," said the emperor.

"He is kind and my friend," cried Wei. The pleading and crying were to no avail. The guards hauled Yin off to the cell to await the emperor's summons.

VIII
Yin is Exiled

At dawn the next morning, Yin was roughly awaken by the guards. "The emperor wants to see you right now," they said.

"But I haven't eaten yet," said Yin.

"You won't need food where you're going," laughed one guard.

The other guard took Yin's arm and pulled him up off the floor. "Time to go lad I'm glad I'm not you this day," said the guard.

They escorted him into a chamber. It was a rather large room with only one seat raised above the floor. "Most likely the emperor's courtroom or war room. Well anyway, it's some type room that isn't a sign of good times to come," thought Yin. The emperor entered and the guards, pulling Yin with them, knelt down and lowered their heads.

"Master Yin come forth," said the emperor.

Yin approached the emperor and halted when he held up his hand.

"Now lad you have done me a grave disservice. You have imposed upon my daughter and I know not what else you did," said Mang.

"I did nothing but talk to her sire," said Yin.

"A guard said he saw you touching her hand what say you about that scoundrel?" asked Mang.

"An innocent brush a mistake is all," replied Yin.

"Nonetheless, you touched a royal princess with your common hand. For this alone beheading is the price," said Mang.

"To talk to her and sit next to her, a double beheading would be in order, if you had two heads," said Mang in an irate voice.

"Since you only have one it will have to do." said Mang.

Mang's face seemed to become redder, with anger, as each minute passed. "When the sun rises on the next day you will be taken to the village center and put to death by beheading," Mang said in a staunch voice.

"Please sire I meant no harm. It was all innocent I swear," pleaded Yin.

"The law is the law," replied Mang.

"Take him away until sunrise tomorrow," Mang said with a flick of a hand.

Neither Mang nor Yin noticed that Wei was hiding behind the side entrance door listening to the proceedings.

"Father you can't do that. He is my friend. It was my fault; I begged him to sit and talk to me," cried Wei.

"Nonsense child, he has clouded your mind for you to say such things," said Mang.

"But it's true father, I swear," replied Wei.

"You are correct sire it was all my fault," shouted Yin not wanting Wei to get into trouble trying to save him.

"See the lad even refutes your claims daughter," said Mang.

"The sentence will be carried out as I decreed."

Wei came forward, tears steaming down her cheeks. "But father I love him," she said crying.

"Ha! Love. You don't know anything of such foolishness. Daughter now back to your room," Mang said. "Guards, off with the boy as I instructed," he bellowed.

"Father if you behead Yin, I will never speak to you again in your lifetime, nor will I ever marry and bear you grandchildren," said Wei now more composed.

"Foolish girl, you will forget this knave soon enough I assure you," said Mang.

"I promise you that what i say is true father," said Wei as she turned her back on Mang.

Meanwhile, the guards had taken Yin to the cell to await his execution time.

Just before sunrise, Yin was yanked from his sleep and dragged to the village center. A man in a hood stood by a rock block. In his hand he held the biggest ax that Yin had ever seen. As the guard was leading Yin to the block, all the onlookers became silent. The people knelt to the ground and bowed. Not knowing what was going on Yin stood straight and looked around. One of the guards yanked Yin down and said "stay put." The emperor had arrived; an unexpected arrival for sure, for the emperor never attended a beheading unless it was a person of great status.

The emperor spoke "I have changed my mind. Although the boy's crime was a grave one, I have decided not to have him beheaded."

A mumbling went though the crowd. Never had they seen the emperor spare anyone.

"Instead, I will banish him to the far corner of the kingdom, never to step foot in this realm again, that is my final word," with this said Mang turned and left.

It seemed to Yin that the remote possibility of Wei carrying out her threat had worried Mang enough for him to change his mind. He matter what the reason Yin was greatful that his life had been spared. spared. At least now he would have a chance to devise a plan that would bring Wei and him together forever.

Yin being exiled by Emperor Mang

IX
Yin's Visit Home

As was the custom of the time, Yin was allowed to return home for five days before the exile was to begin. His mother cried and his father was very upset. Yi offered to go to the emperor and try to persuade him to allow him to take Yin's place but Yin would not hear of it. He had gotten into the trouble on his own and he would have to pay the price for his desires. During the five days, Yin helped Yi prepare a large number of starbursts for the coming events he would be attending.

Yi would have to find another helper for Yin's mother was too frail to travel and carry the boxes.

"I am sorry for the trouble and shame I have brought upon the family," Yin said.

"Be not sorry my son for it is in all of us to follow our desires at some point in life and they always don't turn out the way we hope," said Yi.

Yin's mother busied herself with mending Yin's clothes and preparing supplies for his exile. The Chan family had a great feast the night before Yin was to leave. They talked of old times and what the future would hold.

Yi said "Well, I think that in a few years when Wei is married, the emperor will release you from the exile." Yin said

"She will never marry until I'm released for she will only marry me." Yi replied

"Oh foolish son, her father will have her married off before she turns eighteen for after that she will be at the age that very few will want her."

Yin looked sad as he said, "You'll see father you'll see."

The next morning Yin packed his bags and prepared to head to the far side of the kingdom. His father brought him several bags and handed them to him. "These are the powders for making the colored starburst. You should use them to practice the trade so when you're released you can replace me on at the festivals," said Yi."

Yin thought that he probably wouldn't follow his father's trade but accepted them as an honor to him. "Thank you father. I shall be diligent in my practice," said Yin.

With hugs and good-byes all around Yin left on his trek. "I shall return one day and be a better man and son then you could imagine," said Yin.

X

The Discovery

It took Yin three days to reach the exile village and another day to find a hut to live in. He settled in and began his wait until the day he was released from exile, if that day ever came. Yin tended his small garden, practiced archery and mingled somewhat with the others. But his heart wasn't in it, he long for his darling Wei. Her wonderful smile filled his ever dream. He saw her face in the clouds, the pond and everywhere his looked. Often travelers would pass thorough the village and Yin would ask of the emperor's daughter. He gathered little news from them, for few were privy to the happenings in the palace. Sometimes one would tell him of rumors they heard. One told Yin that he heard the princess was ill, being forlorn for a lost love but he knew little else. On occasion, a messenger from the palace would travel through and often they would bring Yin small notes from Wei. She missed him, she wrote, and has been trying to change her father's mind, but to no avail. Yin would send notes back professing of his undying love for her. He would swear that one day he would return to save her. Time passed slowly, days seemed like years, years seemed like eons and Yin couldn't see an end to his dilemma. One day during the rainy season Yin was sitting on the steps of his hut with a bag of his father's colorings. He took a small sample from the bag and looked at it. In disgust he flung it into the air. "I'll never be a starburst master, for I'll never get out of here," he said to himself.

He sat in despair watching the rain fall, knowing that they were really his heart's tears from missing the lovely Wei. When the sun returned to Yin's amazement a blue streak appeared across the area he had tossed the powder.

Yin discovers the rainbow arc from his star burst powder

The next day it rained again and Yin tossed the powder in the air, when the sun returned a colored streak once more appeared across the area. Yin had a brilliant idea the next time it rained he took a small sack put tiny hole in it, filled it with powder, and tied the sack to an arrow. He shot the arrow in a high arc across the sky and when the sun appeared a great arc of color crossed the sky where his arrow had passed. The next rain, Yin tried two bags and the next, three bags until he had used the seven bags of colors his father had given him. Then Yin came up with an even more brilliant idea. Over the next few days he busied himself with creating a super bow and arrows to match. When it was finished and tested, he knew that he had the tools to let Wei know that he loved her and thought of her always. The next palace messenger that passed by, Yin told him to tell the princess after the next rain to look towards the sky for a sign. Yin would not disclose what the sign would be but told the messenger that she could not miss it and would be delighted. A couple days later, when it rained again, Yin had his equipment already prepared. Using a winch he drew the bow back and placed the arrow on the slot he had made for it. Then with one swing of an ax he cut the cord that held the bow string in place, and sent the arrow soaring across the sky

XI

Wei Sees the Rainbow

Wei waited in great anticipation for the rain to come. The few days she waited seemed to take forever. She would run to the window each morning and look out at the sky.

"Oh I hope it rains today," she would say to her companion.

"You say that every day," replied the companion.

"One day you're sure to be right. Until then, get dressed. Your father is waiting," the companion would say.

The day the rain finally came Wei rushed to her window and sat there for hours waiting for it to cease. After what seemed like an eon or two, the rain stopped and the sun started to emerge. Wei watched the sky with the eagerness of a small child waiting for a candy stick. Then, on the horizon she saw a faint colored bow arcing across the sky. As the sun brightened the colors became more brilliant and she knew this was the sign that Yin had sent word about. How clever of him to think of such a thing. "He must be the brightest of all men for many kingdoms around. No the brightest of men in the universe," she thought to herself.

Yes, this proved he loved her dearly and she knew that she could never marry another no matter what the ramifications.

Wei knew the meaning of the rainbow, but the village people thought it was an omen from the great goddess Yoa telling them that soon the princess Wei would wed and have children. Wei would laugh to herself when she heard the people talking such foolishness. Still, she wished it was true that Yin and she would be able to marry and with her father's blessing. But Mang could be very stubborn especially if he had already made up his mind on a matter. To Wei it appeared Mang had done just that in regards to Yin.

Wei sees the rainbow for the first time.

In defense of her father Wei knew that he only wanted what was best for her. But he didn't always know what was best especially when it came to her heart and feelings. She would bide her time and one day, soon she hoped, he would see it her way. As long as the rainbow crossed the sky after the rains she would hold out for the return of her beloved Yin. She was sure that he would find a way to return from exile and win her father's favor. It had to be true, for no other circumstance would ease the ache she had in her heart and mind. Each day she grew a little more wanting for the one thing that would make them sing with joy, that being the return of Yin to her.

Emperor Mang had no idea how the colors in the sky were caused, some sort of foolish magic he supposed but he grasped onto the villagers belief. He used it to finally declare that Wei was of marrying age and would soon pick a husband. Wei was upset at her father's announcement but knew that the wheels were now in motion for her to be wed soon.

"Father, I hope I get a say in whom I will marry," said Wei.

"Of course child, anything within reason I'm sure," answered her father.

"But mind you it must be soon for the villagers are expecting it," said Mang.

"Oh yes father, I will decide as quickly as I can," answered Wei, knowing that she would stall as long as possible until Yin was free.

Wei found reason after reason to reject her suitors: too small, too big, too poor, too old and too ambitious. Maybe they would overthrow her father and grab the kingdom for themselves and her brothers would then be executed. No,they were not right; she was sure of that. Mang was becoming very impatient at his daughter's excuses and told her she best pick soon or he would do it for her. Wei would always reply "Yes father soon very soon I assure you." Meanwhile, as each rain came, she sat by her window awaiting the bright colored bow that would appear after, the very sign that Yin still loved her.

Yin meanwhile, was still waiting for his pardon from exile for surely the emperor by now must know how Wei felt. As her father, he would have to give in to her wishes at some point in time. Yin kept making the arrows to shoot across the sky. He didn't dare fail, for then Wei might think he stopped loving her. He even got a messenger to go to his father's house and retrieve more powders for he was running low and dared not chance running out. Yin heard from some travelers that the emperor had promised the village that Wei would soon marry, but as of yet she had not picked anyone as a husband. She seemed to be very picky as to who she would marry.

XII
Mang Takes Action

Wei was able to fend of her father's wishes, for a year, making one excuse after another for not picking someone. Once, she even faked illness for several weeks to escape a wealthy prince from the northern kingdom. Yet it was getting harder to think of new reasons and she knew that soon her father's request would turn to demand. But the rainbows were always a source of energy to help her repel her father's demands.

In the early spring of the following year Mang announced that he would hold a contest and the winner would become Wei's husband. This, he felt, was the only way since Wei herself was unable or unwilling to select one from the many that had offered. Wei was devastated and fell into such a depression that even the rainbows had a hard time to lift her spirits.

"I refuse to marry some contest winner," she told her father.

"You have had ample time to choose a husband from the many honorable and prestigious men that have come calling. I can not wait any longer or the villagers will think me a fool," said Mang.

"Let them I wish not to marry for your convenience but for love and a true heart," Wei said.

"Oh, you and your thoughts of love. Love has nothing to do with it. You are of age and it is your duty to do so love or not," answered her father.

"I will not do it never ever," cried Wei.

"We shall see," said Mang.

The word went out that a great contest would be held at the summer dragon festival for the honor to wed the princess Wei. Since the news was not disseminated to his province, Yin was unaware of the great announcement. He kept shooting his rainbow arrows each time it rained and was comfortable that Wei was still safe from marrying another. One day a messenger stopped by. He was in a hurry he said for he had to get to the mountains to retrieve the fur of the winter silk worms to make a suitable dress for the princess.

"A dress? Why would she need a dress of such fine silk?" asked Yin.

"She's to be married come the summer festival," answered the messenger.

"Married to whom?" asked Yin.

"It is not known yet, for the emperor has called for a great contest to determine who shall wed his daughter," said the messenger.

"A contest? How foolish is that?" asked Yin.

"Well, Wei has refused to name a husband, so the emperor decided that this would be the way to choose for her. I assure you he doesn't think it the best way but he feels it is the fairest," said the messenger, then he was off to the mountains for the silk.

XIII

Yin Makes a Plan

Yin knew he had little time. He set straight away to devising a plan to leave his exile and save Wei from her dilemma. He sent the next travel to ask his father to come to the exile village insisting that it was of utmost importance even a matter of life or death. Yin could be dramatic over such things as love.

In three days time, Yi had arrived at the village were Yin was exiled. Yin told his father of the emperor's plan to wed Wei to the winner of some contest.

His father said "Yes I have heard this, the whole kingdom talks of nothing else. Princes and paupers alike are readying for the great ordeal." "There are even funny dressed suitors from beyond the great desert," continued Yi.

"What am I to do?" asked Yin.

"I must find a way to get to the village and save Wei from such a fate," he said.

"You put yourself in great danger if you leave here," said his father.

"That is of no consequence. Father, I must try. I would be less than honorable if I did nothing," said Yin.

"True son, so tell me what is it we can do. Tell me, and I will help the best I can," said Yi.

"But father, you to, will be in great danger for helping. I can not allow it," said Yin.

"You are my son; I will help. Your mother would disown me otherwise, and as for danger, let the fates do as they see fit," replied Yi.

So father and son went to planning the great escapade that would get Yin to the contest to save his beloved Wei. They made plan after plan and none seemed as if it would work. One day a messenger came by and they inquired as to when the great contest would be held.

"It one week's time at the apex of the dragon festival," said the messenger. That leaves us little time father," said Yin in a panic voice.

"Fear not son. We will think of something in time I'm sure," said Yi although his voice held a hint of uncertainty.

As the day approached, Yi became desperate to find a way. He came up with one ridiculous scheme after another. Only his father's calmness kept Yi from doing something rash. Then, it came to them, they would pose as messengers from the kingdom to the North. They would bring gifts for the great wedding, surely no guard would turn away persons bearing the princess gifts. Yes, it would work for few guards even knew what Yin looked like; he had changed a lot in his years of exile. The next day, they packed their stuff, made bags to represent gifts and headed to the village. As luck would have it, it rained the morning that Yin and his dad were to leave. Yin fitted his bow so he could send Wei one last message before he left. This time Yin decided to change two of the color positions hoping Wei would notice and realize that it was a special message that he was on his way.

XIV

The Festival

At her window, Wei awaited the sun to come out so that the rainbow would appear and make her heart happier. At this moment it was saddened with the impending scheme of her father. The rainbow arced across the sky as it had many times before. The villagers thought it a good omen but only Wei noticed that the blue and green were in different places. Her heart jumped nearly out of her body for this could only mean that Yin had a plan. "Such a foolish boy was he, brave but foolish," she thought. She was afraid for him but her heart was too happy for her to worry.

On the day of the festival , at noon, in the great field of contests, the emperor had the festivities stopped and stood to make his announcement.

"Today as you all know is the day that a husband will be picked for my daughter Wei," he said.

"He will be chosen by three contests of skill, for I think one of great skill will also be one of great mind and strength," said Mang.

"In the first contest each contestant will have three shots at the running pig. Those that hit it three times will be allowed to move to the next challenge," said Mang.

"All those wishing to compete come forward and prepare," said the contest master.

There must have been nearly a hundred men and boys who stepped forward, each hoping the prize would be theirs to claim. Among them was a mysterious lad who covered most of his face with a hood.

Of the first group, only twenty hit the mark three times the rest, heads hung low, returned to the crowd.

"For the next part the contestants must figure out a way to free the yak from a net without using any tools but their hands," said the contest master.

"The ones that can do it within the hour will be allowed to the final challenge," he continued.

Twenty yaks were netted up and readied for the contest. It seemed easy enough but the contestants seem to forget that a netted yak can be very ferocious and mean. Of the twenty only two were able to perform the task in the time. One was the prince from the neighboring southern kingdom, which Mang secretly hoped would win, for it would make a nice alliance against the hoards from the North and East. The other was the mysterious lad claiming to be from the northern kingdom. The lad had freed the yak in only ten minutes by luring it to sleep with song, then untied it.

"Surely the prince still would prevail for the lad would be no competition in the final trial," thought Mang.

The final contest was to see who could present the better entertaining shot to a target at the edge of the field. The prince was renowned for his archery and for being an entertainer also. He stepped to the mark and, as if by magic, produced four doves each holding a ribbon. As the prince shot his arrow the doves took off and followed, when the arrow hit the target they swooped in different directions making a flower from the ribbons. The crowded cheered and cheered. Surely no one could beat that, especially a young lad such as stood by the mark now.

Yin asked "Emperor Mang for my final shot may I ask an indulgence?"

"What would that be?" asked the emperor.

"Could I have your balloonist fly above the pathway to the target and on my command dump buckets of water over it?" asked Yin. Although it seemed a strange request Mang agreed and dispatched his balloonist to the stations Yin had asked for. Yin moved back about one hundred paces more and gave the command for the balloonist to drop the water.

"It wasn't rain but it would have to do," thought Yin.

The one good thing was it would dry quickly and the effect he hoped for should be almost instantaneous. Yin drew back his bow and released the arrow. Nothing seemed different just an arrow, with some small bags attached, which soon found the target. The crowd stood dumbfounded what sort of entertainment was this? Truly, anyone could shoot an arrow. The emperor stood up and was about to declare the prince the winner when to his amazement several streaks of color appeared and formed a perfect rainbow across the area where the water had been poured. For several seconds no one said anything, all were very awestruck. Then a voice could be heard and then clapping and soon all the people joined in. Mang stood staring in amazement, unable to speak. Soon he regained his composure and joined in the applause. "This is a very impressive display," thought Mang.

As fast as the thought had entered Mang's mind it was as quickly dismissed. This wasn't what he wanted to see, he was hoping for complete failure by the lad. Mang was confused as to how he was to declare the prince the winner when it was clear the crowd approved of the lad.

Yin's final shot of the contest produced a rainbow

XV
Wei Prevails

Wei knew right away who the lad was. She shivered with excitement at the performance of her beloved Yin. The crowd continued their wild dancing and shouting. They not only cheered but gave the lad the ultimate recognition by banging pot and pans and ringing bells.

Her father spoke to the contest master and said "Against the villagers wishes I want you to pronounce the prince the winner."

"But sire never has a contest outcome been overturned by the master," said the contest master.

"It will be this time. You have my orders carry them out," said Mang.

"As you desire," said the master. He was about to make the announcement when Wei said to her father

"You chose the contest and the prize. Now you must honor the results or the demons of the night will surely have their way with you."

"But daughter, I can't allow a mere peasant, a lad at that, to marry you. It would be against the royal tradition," said Mang.

"Nonetheless, father, the rules have to be upheld if you wish your subjects to honor you as just and fair," said Wei.

The emperor raised his hand and stopped the contest master and said "It is not as I wish, that the lad won. But since it is your wish, then I hold back my urge to change the winner and honor your choice. The boy is the winner."

The crowd went wilder than before and the prince in disgust started to storm off, tripped and landed in fresh yak droppings. This brought an even louder cheers and laughter from the crowd.

The emperor motioned the boy to come forth.

"You have, with honor and distinction, earned the prize of my daughter's hand in marriage. Remove your hood and let me see who has claimed such an honor."

Yin removed the hood and the crowd gasped as the emperor's face became ferocious with anger. "Guards take this scoundrel to the dungeon," he roared "What ever possessed you to venture here knowing your ultimate fate?" asked Mang.

"It was my love for your daughter, sire," answered Yin.

"Love," scoffed Mang.

"Love has only been your death warrant I'm afraid lad," said Mang.

Wei spoke in a low tone that only her father could hear "Father how would it look if you killed your daughter's husband before they were even married. Besides he is my one true love and if I can't marry him I will throw myself into the fire pit."

Again Mang was at the mercy of his daughter. He could not take a chance that she would carry out her threat. He shook his head and spoke again. "My daughter is right. The lad has won the contest and, as much as I want to send him to the dungeon, I must honor the win," proclaimed Mang.

" The wedding will be held three week hence," said Mang to the approving roar of the crowd.

XVI
The Rainbow's Meaning Revealed

Wei and her escorts spent most of the week readying for the wedding, as did the people of the village. There was much to be done: the hall to get ready, the food to gather, entertainment to arrange and a host of guests to send messages of invite to. Most important was the finishing of Wei's wedding dress. The silk was spun and the dressmakers spent day and night getting it right. The fear of the emperor's wrath seemed to make mere mortals do whatever it took to make things right. "It is sure to be the biggest gala ever seen in the kingdom or the universe for that matter," thought the villagers.

Yin had little to do. His clothes were readied by his mother. His father was the go-between for the wedding planers and the family. So Yin just sat around a lot, worrying if he was ready for such a step. But no matter, his love for Wei and hers for him would get them through any trouble spots. To pass the idle time, Yin worked in his father starburst shop preparing the burst for the wedding's evening celebration. He also prepared several arrows to be used so Wei would know beyond a doubt that his love was true. Yin also would sneak to the palace wall and Wei would be waiting for him. They would talk about the future.

One day Wei asked "Yin I've seen the wonderful rainbow you created each time it rained and I know it represents your love for me. Why so many colors? I would have loved it with just one."

Yin thought for a moment trying to arrange the thoughts in his head so they would come out of his mouth correctly. "Well, I had so many because each one of them represents a unique promise of love from me to you," he said.

"What sort of promises?" asked Wei.

Then Yin began to explain the meaning of each color. **"The blue is the promise of unconditional love between us. The red is the promise of oneness of the you and me. Green is the promise of truth forever in all things. The yellow is the promise of trust no matter what the winds say. The color violet is the promise of compassionate caring whether one is well or sick. Orange is the promise of passion to be lived until the end. The last is the pale color that represents an endless love now and forever, even beyond the mortal realm. These are the promises represented by the rainbow colors I sent each time the rains came and will send to you each moment of our lives," he said.**

"Oh Yin that is so wonderfully I must be allowed to recite it at the wedding for all to hear and know what a great person you are," said Wei. Yin tried to talk Wei out of reciting the meanings but she insisted and he could not refuse.

XVII
The Wedding

The wedding day came and all went
well. Wei told the villagers of the true meaning of the
rainbow they had seen after the rains. The villagers
were truly happy and some of the women wept openly
at such devotion. Some of the men wept inside wishing
they had been the inventor of such a devotion. The
villagers cheered and sang. Yi displayed one of his
greatest starburst shows ever. The two families feasted
and enjoyed each other's company. The smaller
children ran around, played, giggled and ate. Yin and
Wei danced and greeted a zillion guests. Nobles from
other clans to the East and West, their families and
friends, and the many village people that attended all
wanted to see and greet Yin and Wei, to wish them
well in their future. The women gave Wei special
advice on how to have many healthy children. They
laughed and sang old traditional wedding songs. Wei
played a song on her harp, which surprised Yin; he
didn't know she played a musical instrument. There
were more wishes of happiness and well being given by
the many distinguished guests as well as family
members. The villagers seemed very pleased with the
choice Wei had made for a husband. It was a most
wonderful time. Mang, seeing how happy the villagers
were, began to think that maybe his daughter was

wiser in the matters of love than he had given her credit for.

Wei and Yin are married

XVIII
Yin and Wei Settle In

Mang offered Yin a position in the Emperor's army as a teacher of archery, but Yin refused the tempting offer.

"Why would one refuse such a distinguished position?" asked Mang.

"I would have to travel to the far reaches of the kingdom to do the job and, as such, would be gone from my beloved Wei too much," answered Yin.

"We wish to live a simple life in the country farming and raising animals," continued Yin.

"It will be good to raise our children in the quiet countryside and they will be able to learn the value of both worlds: yours, Emperor Mang, and ours. They will be well educated in all facets of life this way," said Yin.

"My daughter a pheasant that's out of the question," stammered Mang.

"But father we could be the royal farm raising goods to be used in the feast you have ever year. It would be a great honor for us," chimed in Wei.

"Well what about the grandchildren?" asked Mang.

"They will visit you often and, when old enough, they will come to the palace for their schooling, returning home to help with summer planting and fall harvest," laughed Wei. "Don't worry you'll get plenty of chance to spoil them," chuckled Wei.

Emperor Mang knew his daughter had outwitted him again and relented to their request. The villagers seemed pleased that the couple would be more like them than anyone from the royal family had ever been.

Yin and Wei were given a place in the southern sector and Yin was made an ambassador of the kingdom. He also was made the official starburst master after his father passed away, although he only plied the trade at festivals at Mang's palace. Wei helped him sometimes but soon he was teaching his sons the trade. They lived long and happy lives and had many children. And at night, when the children craved for Wei to tell them a story, she would often tell them of the young lad that invented the rainbow to let his true love know he still loved her. She never told them it was their father but after many recitations they figured it out. The children would just sit and listen to the tale as if it was a new one being told instead of one they had heard a hundred or so times before. They never grew tried of its sentimental portrayal of their parent's love. The story became folklore throughout the kingdom and beyond. Young girls sat by their windows after the rains hoping to see the rainbow and insist it was for them from some great admirer. Others took it as an omen that all was well with the world, and that the kingdom would be forever prosperous. But the two old folks that sat on the steps knew the true meaning. They would smile and hold hands until it had disappeared.

So when the rains come followed by a rainbow you may think of it what you will. A scientific meaning, a spiritual one or some other omen of the universe. But for a moment stop, and remember the story of Yin Chan and Wei Wu and the seven promises of love that it represented to them.

Wei and Yin always enjoyed the rainbow

www.ingramcontent.com/pod-product-compliance
Lightning Source LLC
Chambersburg PA
CBHW020340130626
46549CB00003B/1223